Alpha-Mania Adventures

PIRATES: BOOK TWO

Slomo's Secret Treasure

WRITTEN BY JENNIFER MAKWANA, B. ED., ECE
ILLUSTRATED BY JALISA HENRY

Collect all five books in the *Alpha-Mania® Adventures* Pirate Series!

BOOK 1
Captain Ray and the Rhyming Pirates: A Rhyming Book

BOOK 2
Slomo's Secret Treasure: A Blending Book

BOOK 3
The Fantastic Floating Feast: An Alliteration Book

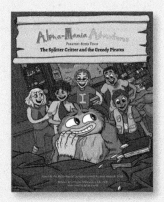

BOOK 4
The Splitter Critter and the Greedy Pirates: A Segmenting Book

BOOK 5
The Great Riddle Race: A Sound Manipulation Book

ruth rumack's
LEARNING SPACE

Ruth Rumack's Learning Space
720 Spadina Avenue, Suite 504
Toronto, Ontario M5S 2T9
www.ruthrumack.com
www.rumackresources.com
www.alpha-mania.com

Book and Cover Design: Kathleen Fasciano and Jalisa Henry

Executive in Charge of Production: Evan Brooker

ISBN: 978-0994763754

MORE THAN A STORYBOOK!

The *Alpha-Mania*® *Adventures* series is designed to develop **phonological awareness** and **phonics** in young children, the first two of the five essential components of reading (phonological awareness, phonics, vocabulary, fluency, and comprehension). Research on early reading strategies shows that phonological awareness, especially when combined with phonics, is an important foundation in helping children learn to read, and one of the best predictors of future reading success.*

PHONOLOGICAL AWARENESS is the ability to hear and manipulate the sounds of spoken language. This includes five skills: rhyming, blending, alliteration, segmenting, and sound manipulation.

Phonological awareness comes alive through the interactive and exciting pirate story! Practice a different skill in each of the five books, then play the fun, multisensory activities provided to reinforce the skill.

PHONICS is the relationship between the sounds of spoken language and the symbols (or letters) that represent those sounds. For example: *"This letter is a T. It makes the sound /t/."*

Play a fun phonics activity as you read! The scroll at the bottom of the story pages indicates hidden objects or letters for children to hunt for within the colorful illustrations. (Answer key on page 38)

The phonological awareness focus of *Slomo's Secret Treasure* is **blending.** Blending is practiced by listening to a sequence of individual sounds or sound parts, and combining those sounds to form a word. It can be practiced in multiple ways: Combining the two parts of a compound word (base...ball becomes *baseball*), combining syllables (ba...na...na becomes *banana*) and combining individual sounds (sss...uuu...nnn becomes *sun*).

In this book, the Alpha-Maniacs meet a slow-speaking sloth that pauses between word parts or stretches the individual sounds in words. If word parts are separated by an ellipsis (...), this indicates you should pause between each part. For example, when the sloth says the word *someone*, it will be written as *some...one*, and you should pause between the *some* and *one*. The individual sounds that need to be stretched will be repeated in the spelling. For example, the word *map* will be written as *mmmaaap*. This indicates that you should stretch the /m/ sound and the /a/ sound, but not the /p/ sound. (Certain "quick" sounds should not be stretched – see Appendix A for a complete explanation of quick and stretchy sounds.) Sometimes the story will ask the reader questions, for example, *"Where do the Alpha- Maniacs need to go next?"* You may need to repeat some of the stretched words in the text so that children have the chance to practice blending the words on their own. You may find it somewhat difficult to read initially, but stick with it. Children will enjoy your slow-talking sloth voice, so take your time and have fun with it!

For more information on the research or how to get Alpha-Mania® *books and lessons into your school, please visit www.alpha-mania.com*

Letter Lagoon is a magical place. It's a place where towering cliffs, mysteriously carved with letters, rise out of the crystal blue water. It's a place where adventure hides behind every twisted tree and rugged rock. It's a place where you never know what might happen next.

It's also the home of the Alpha-Maniacs.

Alex, Eddie, Izzy, Olly, and Umber call themselves the Alpha-Maniacs because they love letters! In fact, they love letters so much, even their shirts have letters on them.

Can you guess who is who?

Nearly a month had passed since the Alpha-Maniacs' first encounter with real pirates.

"Do you think Captain Ray and his crew will find the treasure on their map?" wondered Izzy as the Alpha-Maniacs strolled along the beach looking for seashells.

"Of course they'll find it," Eddie insisted. "We taught them everything we know."

"I wish we were the ones out searching for treasure," sighed Alex. "We could sure use a little adventure around here today."

Find the letters that these pictures begin with...

"You want adventure, Alex? I'll race you to that cave over there," Olly yelled. Alex dropped her shells and raced after him.

"Watch out for that log!" Umber called out just before Olly and Alex landed in a heap in the sand.

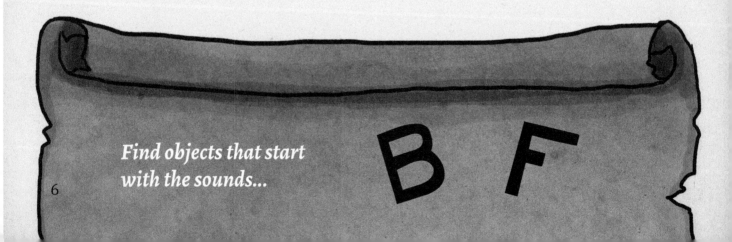

Find objects that start with the sounds...

B F

When the others caught up to them, Olly and Alex were staring in disbelief at the sand.

"What is it? Are you guys okay?" inquired Izzy.

Everyone leaned in to see a weathered old scroll poking out from under the driftwood.

Find the letters that these pictures begin with...

"Is that what I think it is?" Eddie stammered.

Umber unrolled the scroll. "Well, if you think it's a treasure map, upon my initial inspection, it does appear to have some of the elements that are typical to a map of..."

"Of course it's a treasure map, Umber!" Olly cut in.

"There's something very familiar about this map." Izzy noted.

"You're right, Izzy," Alex agreed. "I just don't know what it could be."

Suddenly, Eddie snatched up the map and held it out in front of him.

"I don't believe it! This is a map of Alpha-Mania Island! See, those are the cliffs straight ahead, and this right here is the Letter Lagoon."

"Eddie's right! Eddie's right!" Umber squealed with excitement.

"Well, what are we standing around for?" Alex piped in. "Let's follow the path!"

"Wait!" called Izzy as the others started off down the beach. "Shouldn't we gather some supplies?"

The Alpha-Maniacs stopped in their tracks. As usual, they knew Izzy was right.

"I'll grab the shovels," yelled Olly.

"And I'll get our pirate hats," called Alex.

"Don't forget the swords!" Eddie called after her.

The Alpha-Maniacs quickly loaded up their turtle wagon and set off down the path.

Find the letters that these pictures begin with...

The Alpha-Maniacs easily found the location of the X on the map. They had explored nearly every inch of the island.

"Nothing looks out of place here," remarked Izzy.

"Just start digging!" shouted Olly as he flung the shovels from the wagon.

Suddenly, a strange, deep voice echoed from the treetop.

"Ex...cuse me," murmured the voice. "Is some...one there?"

Find objects that start with the sounds...

H A

"Who said that?" asked Alex looking up.

"I diiid," answered the voice.

"Who are you?" demanded Eddie, puffing out his chest.

A furry gray sloth slid slowly down one of the tree branches.

"Mmmy nnnaaammme is Ssslllommmo the Ssslllloth."

The Alpha-Maniacs looked bewildered.

"I think we're gonna need a translator," announced Olly. "This sloth speaks soooooo slowly!"

Can you help? What is the sloth's name?

"I see you child...ren found my mmmaaap," Slomo muttered. "I left it in...side a piece of drift...wood."

The Alpha-Maniacs stared blankly at the sloth. This was going to be a *loooooong* day.

"Is there treasure buried here?" Olly asked, a little impatiently.

"There uuusssed to beee," slurred Slomo. "But I mmmoooved it."

"I don't understand a single thing this sloth says," grumbled Eddie. "How are we going to find this treasure?"

"It's easy, Eddie," explained Umber. "We just have to blend the sounds together to figure out the words he is saying."

"Sssooo, do you want to fffiiinnnd the treasure thennn?" inquired Slomo.

"We sure do!" squealed Alex. She was starting to catch on to the sloth's slow speech.

18

"Llliiiiisssten closely," continued Slomo, "First you mmmuuussst fol...low the rrrocks until you see a nnnessst."

"Follow the who until we see a what?" asked Olly.

"Listen," explained Umber, "He says it slowly –*rrrocks* – but we say it fast – *rocks*. Let's try the other one together. Slomo said 'nnnessst' so we say..."

"Nest!" shouted the Alpha-Maniacs.

"Don't worry, Olly." Umber stated confidently. "I know what to do."

With Umber leading the way, the Alpha-Maniacs soon arrived at a giant nest in a tiny tree.

"How do we get up there?" wondered Alex.

"C'mon Umber, I'll give you a boost," piped Eddie.

Umber groaned. He was always getting hoisted into unusual places.

Umber reached into the giant nest and pulled out another scroll.

"It's another note!" Umber cheered as he tumbled into a pile of moss.

Find the letters that these pictures begin with...

As Umber brushed himself off, Alex read the note:

"Now follow the sssuuunnn until you rrreeeach,
The cllliiifffsss beyond the rrrocky beeeach"

Can you say it fast? Point to where the Alpha-Maniacs need to go next.

*Find objects that start
with the sounds...*

Y N

When they reached the cliffs, the Alpha-Maniacs split up and began to search the rocky ground.

"I've got it!" announced Izzy, holding up another scroll.

She straightened her glasses and read the note:

"The letter S will lead you to
A lllaaake of many fffiiish
Buried in the sssaaannnd beside
Is where you'll get your wish."

Where do the Alpha-Maniacs need to go next?"

Find the letters that these pictures begin with...

With the help of some good blending, the Alpha-Maniacs arrived at the lake.

The excited Alpha-Maniacs dug furiously until Alex's shovel made a large bang.

"Over here! Over here!" Alex shrieked.

The other Alpha-Maniacs helped Alex pull out a small but heavy chest. Eddie used his shovel to pry it open.

Find objects that start with the sounds... K U

Inside the chest, five gold crowns dotted with shimmering rubies, glimmering emeralds, and sparkling diamonds sat atop a sea of gleaming, gold coins.

As the Alpha-Maniacs stared in disbelief, Slomo slunk down a nearby tree trunk.

"Ex...cell...ent work child...ren. You have passed my test. You are worthy pro...tec...tors of my treasure."

"What do you mean, Slomo?" inquired Izzy.

"I've been search...ing for someone to help guard my treasure. You ssseee, I'm an old ssslllloth and I'm too ssslllow to keep mmmooovvving it."

"But why do you want to move it?" wondered Olly aloud. "Why not just keep it?"

Find the letters that these pictures begin with...

"Well, there are two mmmaaapsss to this treasure. I have one, but the other fell into the hands of some greedy pirates. If I don't keep mmmooovvving the treasure, the greedy pirates will sure...ly fffiiinnnd it."

"We'll protect it! You can count on us, Slomo," assured Eddie.

"And in ex...change," answered Slomo, "I will give you half the treasure once we know it's sssaaafffe from the greedy pirates."

"Wow! Half of this treasure will be ours? You've got yourself a deal, sloth!" exclaimed Olly.

"Do you guys hear something?" Alex whispered.

The Alpha-Maniacs dropped their shovels and listened. A faint noise echoed off the nearby cliffs. It sounded like singing.

"That's a pirate song!" declared Eddie as the noise grew louder.

"Pirates?" Umber stammered nervously. "Which pirates?"

"Quick, bury the treasure!" shouted Olly, jumping into action.

The Alpha-Maniacs hurriedly buried Slomo's treasure and raced to the beach. An enormous, extravagant ship was heading straight for Letter Lagoon.

"Quick, hide over here!" yelled Eddie, ducking behind a giant boulder.

The Alpha-Maniacs watched nervously as the mighty ship dropped its anchor. All of a sudden, an owl flew from the crow's nest and landed in front of the Alpha-Maniacs.

"I know that owl!" declared Alex. "He's a part of Captain Ray's crew!"

"Ahoy thar, mateys!" bellowed a deep voice from the ship. "Have we got a story for ye fine landlubbers!"

The Alpha-Maniacs breathed a sigh of relief. Captain Ray and his crew had returned, just like they said they would. Slomo's treasure was safe...for now.

Find objects that start with the sounds...

L J

BONUS ACTIVITIES
Blending Activities

Below are some quick **blending** activities that you can play with your child. Blending games are excellent ways to introduce your child to the idea that words are made up of individual sounds, which lays the foundation for reading and spelling skills down the road.

Head to Toe

To Play:
This game allows your child to practice blending syllables. Syllables are the parts of words that consist of a single, uninterrupted sound. For example, the word *dinosaur* has three syllables: *di-no-saur*.

With your hands on your head, say the first syllable aloud (See list below - syllables are separated with dashes.) As you bend down to touch your toes, say the final syllable of the word. When the word contains three syllables, touch your head for the first syllable, your hips for the second syllable, and your toes for the final syllable. Have your child repeat your actions and then try to blend the syllables to call out the correct word.

drive-way	*bath-tub*	*rock-et*	*chick-en*	*ham-bur-ger*
pine-cone	*air-port*	*pi-rate*	*ten-nis*	*com-pu-ter*
break-fast	*eye-brow*	*din-ner*	*fam-i-ly*	*el-e-phant*

Blending Slide

To Play:
Use magnetic letters or other letter shapes to spell easily blended words (See list below.) Arrange the letters in a diagonal line to look like a slide. Have your child use a stuffed toy to "slide" down the letters, making the sound for each letter as the toy slides past it. At the bottom of the slide, have your child try to blend the sounds together to call out the word. If necessary, assist your child by helping to make the sounds for each letter.

sad	*fed*	*vet*	*men*	*sit*	*mop*	*fun*	*mix*
map	*red*	*fit*	*net*	*fin*	*rat*	*lad*	*nap*
lip	*not*	*log*	*rub*	*leg*	*sun*	*sub*	*run*

Find it Fast

To Play:
As you flip through the book with your child, call out the name of an object on the page by stretching the individual sounds. Have your child point to the object as quickly as he or she can. Choose objects from the following list as they contain stretchy sounds that are easier to blend. Remember: Only hold the sounds that are written multiple times. Do not hold final sounds like /ck/, /p/, /t/, etc.

Sun (Say "Sssssssuuuuuunnnnnn")

Leaves (Say "Lllllleeeeeeavvvvvves")

Nail (Say "Nnnnnnaaaaaailllllll")

Fish (Say "Fffffffiiiiiish")

Map (Say "Mmmmmmaaaaaap")

Snake (Say "Sssssssnnnnnnaaaaaake")

Flag (Say "Fffffflllllllaaaaaag")

Feet (Say "Ffffffeeeeeeeeeet")

Slomo Says "Say It Fast"

To Play:
This game allows your child to practice blending compound words, syllables, and individual sounds. Pretend to be Slomo the Sloth and say words very "ssslllowly". Your child will then have to say it fast. Start with compound words, then move on to syllables, followed by two-phoneme words, three-phoneme words, and finally four-phoneme words. Remember to pause at the breaks in compound words, between syllables, and to hold only the individual sounds that are written multiple times. Do not hold final sounds such as /ck/, /p/, /g/, and /t/.

Compound Words:	Syllables:	Individual Sounds (Phonemes):
neck-lace	ro-bot	**Two-Phoneme Words:**
in-side	pup-pet	aaaaaat (at)
base-ball	mu-sic	uuuuuup (up)
door-knob	win-dow	zzzzzzoo (zoo)
bed-time	ba-by	**Three-Phoneme Words:**
foot-print	can-dy	rrrrrraaaaaake (rake)
hair-cut	cu-cum-ber	vvvvvvaaaaaannnnnn (van)
grape-fruit	um-brel-la	sssssssiiiiiit (sit)
pan-cake	Sat-ur-day	**Four-Phoneme Words:**
play-ground	fan-tas-tic	fffffflllllliiiiiip (flip)
rain-bow	kin-der-gar-ten	ssssssslllllliiiiiide (slide)
shoe-lace	in-for-ma-tion	ffffffaaaaaasssssst (fast)

Phonics Activities

Phonics activities help your child learn both the names of letters and the sounds they make. Have a set of alphabet letters on hand so that you can reinforce the symbol that each sound represents. This could be magnetic letters, alphabet puzzle pieces, alphabet flashcards, or any letters your child can hold. Playing with three-dimensional letters will help your child better understand the concept of letters as symbols for sounds.

Musical Letters

Set-up:
Lay out about 6-8 different alphabet letters in a large circle on the floor. Choose an area where you have room to spread out and access to music.

To Play:
Have your child stand on one of the letters. Review each letter on the floor by saying the name of the letter and the sound it makes. (*"This is the letter T, it makes the sound /t/."*) Start the music and have your child march around the circle, stepping on each letter. After a short time, stop the music and instruct your child to stop on the nearest letter. Have your child say the name of the letter and the sound it makes. You can also get your child to name something that begins with that sound. Once your child is successful, start the music again and continue. Try to ensure that your child has a chance to practice each letter in the circle.

X Marks the Spot Tic Tac Toe

Set-up:
Print a different letter of the alphabet on nine sheets of paper. Lay the papers out in a 3 by 3 grid pattern on the floor. Make large X's out of two different colors of construction paper. You will need five of each color. You will also need a soft toy for throwing.

To Play:
This game is played like the classic Tic Tac Toe, but with only X's. Take turns tossing a soft toy onto the grid of letters. When it lands, the player must say the name and sound of the letter where the toy landed. If correct, the player puts a colored X over the paper. If the soft toy misses the grid, or lands on a letter that is already taken, the player may throw again. The goal of the game is to "mark the spot" by placing three X's in a row, either vertically, horizontally, or diagonally.

APPENDIX A – GUIDE TO LETTER SOUNDS

• There are two main types of sounds (also called phonemes) in the English language: voiced sounds and unvoiced sounds.

• Voiced sounds occur when the vocal chords vibrate in order to produce the sound. To test this, put your fingers gently against your throat below your chin. As you say a voiced sound, you should feel a gentle vibration against your fingers.

• Unvoiced sounds (also called whisper sounds) do not use the vocal chords. For an unvoiced sound, put your fingers a short distance from your mouth. As you say an unvoiced sound, you should feel a slight puff of air against your fingers. Unvoiced sounds are often incorrectly pronounced as voiced sounds. This results in the vowel sound /uh/ following the letter sound, which is incorrect. For example, the letter P should sound like a whisper or puff of air (/p/, not /puh/).

• Sounds can also be "quick" or "stretchy." Stretchy sounds are those that should be held when pronounced (/mmmm/). Quick sounds should not be held (/t/).

The following chart illustrates the voiced and unvoiced sounds along with the quick and stretchy sounds.

Voiced		Unvoiced	
Quick	Stretchy	Quick	Stretchy
b (/b/ as in bed)	a (/aaaa/ as in apple)	c (/c/ as in cat)	f (/ffff/ as in find)
d (/d/ as in dog)	e (/eeee/ as in egg)	h (/h/ as in hat)	s (/ssss/ as in sun)
g (/g/ as in go)	i (/iiii/ as in igloo)	k (/k/ as in kite)	
j (/j/ as in jet)	l (/llll/ as in lion)	p (/p/ as in pet)	
q (/kw/ as in quit)	m (/mmmm/ as in map)	t (/t/ as in time)	
w (/w/ as in wet)	n (/nnnn/ as in net)	x (/ks/ as in box)	
y (/y/ as in yellow)	o (/oooo/ as in octopus)		
	r (/rrrr/ as in rock)		
	u (/uuuu/ as in umbrella)		
	v (/vvvv/ as in van)		
	z (/zzzz/ as in zoo)		

ABOUT THE AUTHORS

Jennifer Makwana is a certified teacher at Ruth Rumack's Learning Space, an educational support company based in Toronto, Canada. Jennifer has a Bachelor of Arts (Hons.), a Bachelor of Education, and a diploma in Early Childhood Education. Since 2008, she has instructed and expanded the Alpha-Mania® program at Ruth Rumack's Learning Space. Jennifer lives in Toronto with her husband and two children.

Ruth Rumack is the founder and executive director of education of Ruth Rumack's Learning Space. She has a Bachelor of Arts (Hons.) in Psychology and a Bachelor of Education. Ruth created the Alpha-Mania® program in 1996 with the aim of introducing emergent readers to the magic and excitement of the alphabet and phonological awareness. This series brings the Alpha-Mania® program to life through the adventures of the Alpha-Maniacs. Ruth lives in Toronto with her husband and two children.

FIND THE HIDDEN OBJECTS ANSWER KEY

Pages 4-5 – R is hidden in the two small trees beside the treehouses; M is in the sky.
Pages 6-7 – B objects: *bucket, bird, bananas*; F objects: *frog, fish, flamingo*
Pages 8-9 – D is in the water at the shoreline; P is hidden in the blue log.
Pages 12-13 – T is the handle of the shovel in the ground; E is hidden in the trunk of a tree.
Pages 14-15 – H objects: *hippo, hammer, hat*; A objects: *ant, alligator, apple, ax*
Pages 20-21 – C is a cloud in the sky; Q is dug-up sand on the ground.
Pages 22-23 – Y objects: *yacht, yogurt, yarn*; N objects: *nails, nose, numbers*
Pages 24-25 – S is the rope lying among the rocks; V is the reddish-colored plant near the water.
Pages 26-27 – K objects: *kangaroo, kayak, kite*; U objects: *umbrella, underwear*
Pages 28-29 – W is in the blue tree; G is dug-up sand on the ground.
Pages 32-33 – L objects: *log, lobster, ladder*; J objects: *jellyfish, jet, jug*